SARAH LEAN's fascination with animals began
when she was aged eight and a stray cat walked
in the back door and decided to adopt her.
As a child she wanted to be a writer and used
to dictate stories to her mother, until she bought
a laptop of her own several years ago and decided
to type them herself. She loves her garden, art,
calligraphy and spending time outdoors. She lives
in Dorset and shares the space around her desk
with her dogs, Harry and Coco.

www.sarahlean.co.uk

Also by Sarah Lean

Tiger Days and the Secret Cat

For older readers:

A Dog Called Homeless

A Horse for Angel

The Forever Whale

Jack Pepper

Hero

Harry and Hope

TIGER DAYS

DAYS

and the midnight foxes

SARAH LEAN

Illustrations by Anna Currey

HarperCollins *Children's Books*

First published in Great Britain by HarperCollins *Children's Books* in 2016
HarperCollins *Children's Books* is a division of HarperCollins*Publishers* Ltd,
1 London Bridge Street, London, SE1 9GF

The HarperCollins website address is: www.harpercollins.co.uk

1

Text © Sarah Lean 2016
Illustrations © Anna Currey 2016

ISBN 978-0-00-816573-4

Printed and bound in England by Clays Ltd, St Ives plc

MIX
Paper from
responsible sources
FSC **FSC™ C007454**
www.fsc.org

Find out more about HarperCollins and the environment at
www.harpercollins.co.uk/green

For Sophie

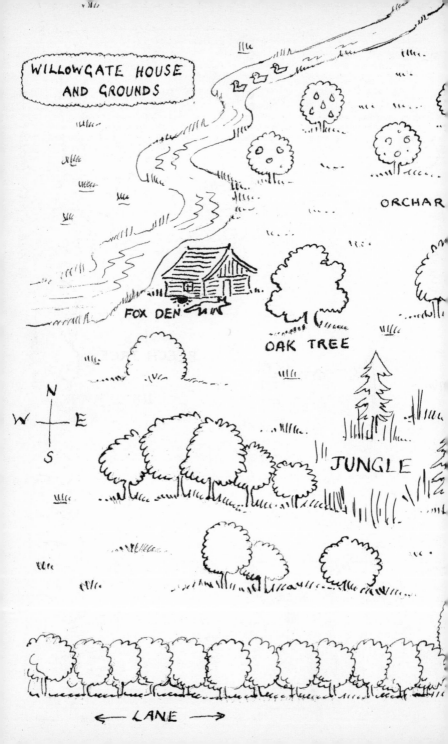

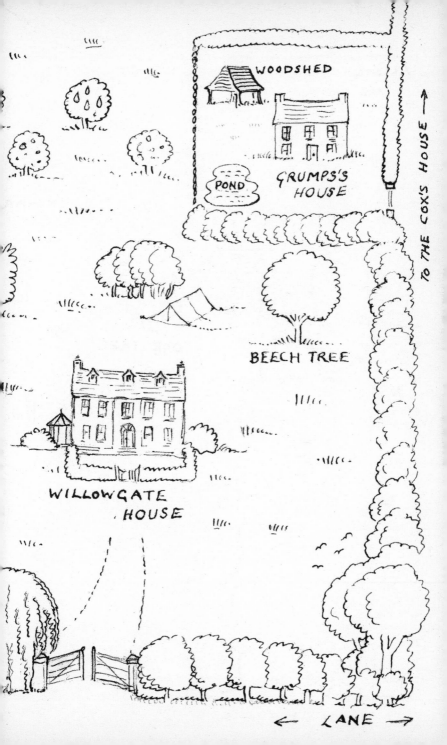

Chapter 1

Where is Holly?

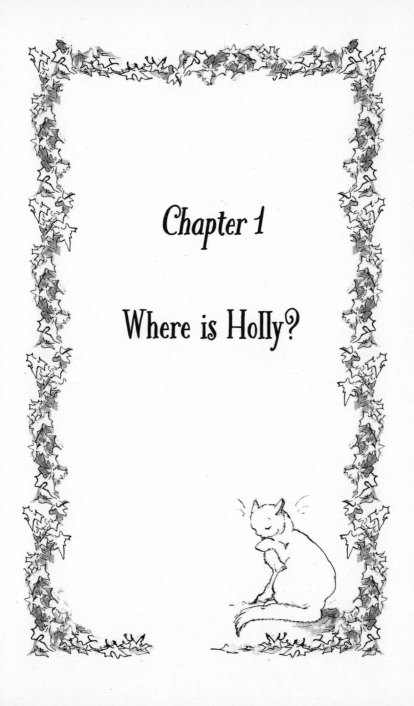

Tiger Days loved tigers. She often
wore tiger-print pyjamas, socks
and slippers and used to spend all her
time indoors drawing pictures of tigers.
Ever since she'd been to stay with her
grandmother, May Days, at her new
house, Tiger was beginning to be more
adventurous. May Days used to live on a
wildlife reserve in Africa but now lived
in a large old house in the countryside,

called Willowgate House. Even now, she sometimes looked after animals that were in need of helping hands. There were lots of repairs to be made at Willowgate, and while the house was being fixed up, May Days and Tiger slept in a tent in the great, unexplored garden.

It was spring, warm and bright, and Tiger was on her way to visit her grandmother but there was a long journey in the car first. Tiger was eager to arrive and see May Days again, as there was still so much to find out about each other.

Excitement swirled in Tiger's tummy as she thought about her grandmother and her new friend Tom, who often stayed with his grandfather next door. Tiger was also looking forward to seeing Holly Days – a white cat who had made her home at Willowgate even before May Days had moved in. She was the kind of cat that did as she pleased and Tiger thought of Holly as belonging to the house, rather than to anyone in particular. Holly had a mind of her own and was quite in charge of herself, but Tiger and the cat had become firm friends during Tiger's last stay.

The car pulled up at the end of the drive, where Tiger had last seen Holly. Obviously Holly wasn't still sitting there, but when Tiger jumped out of the car to open the gate she looked around, hoping

the cat was nearby. There was no sign of
Holly, but May Days was already jogging
down the drive to greet them. Tiger smiled
and ran to meet her grandmother, while
Dad drove up the drive.

"May Days!" said Tiger as the two of
them flung their arms round each other.

"I'm so happy to see you all over again," said May Days, planting a big kiss on Tiger's cheek. The garden smelled of new grass and warm breezes and Tiger hoped she'd find everything else just as before.

In the kitchen, Mr Days had lots to talk about with his mother over gallons of tea, which Tiger didn't mind too much as she was now desperate to find the cat.

"Where's Holly?" she said.

"That cat is still a bit of a mystery," May Days said. "Why don't you go and see if you can find her?"

Holly was not in any of the rooms

downstairs, or hiding in any of the chimneys, or behind any doors. She wasn't upstairs in the bath, or in the bedrooms, or inside the cupboard with the lift in the wall where Tiger had first discovered her. Outside, Holly was not in the porch, nor sitting on the windowsills, nor in the tent.

Tiger called and called but no blossom-white cat came padding through the garden. Tiger anxiously went to her grandmother with empty news and worrying fears.

"What if something terrible has happened to her?" Tiger said, in the comfort of her grandmother's arms.

Every day May Days left out a bowl of food for Holly and the next day it would

be empty, even though May Days didn't
always see the cat.

"You know what Holly is like," May
Days reassured Tiger. "She suddenly turns
up, just like that, looking quite content.
That cat certainly knows how to look after
herself and I'm sure
she'll come when
she's ready."

Before long it was
time for Tiger's dad
to return home.

"What if Holly
doesn't come?" Tiger
said quietly, with a
tremble.

"Don't give up so soon," said Dad, giving her a final, *final* hug. "There might be a completely new adventure waiting for you."

"Are there any poorly animals we need to look after?" Tiger sniffed, holding May Days' hand as she waved goodbye to her dad.

"Not this time," said May Days, and then explained that the builders were coming the next day to fix the chimneys on the roof. "In the meantime, keep your eyes wide open. You never know what else you might find."

To help feel more at home, Tiger unpacked her case in the tent. Colourful striped rugs from Africa covered the ground and the tent smelled of dried grasses and faraway. There were two camp beds, puffy with sleeping bags and blankets, and Tiger put her pyjamas under the pillow of the one where she'd sleep. A rope was strung from one end of the tent to

the other, hung with gas lamps for night-time, coat hangers for clothes, a torch for visiting the outdoor bathroom, and a pair of May Days' shoes tied by the laces. Tiger sat on the end of her bed where Holly used to sleep, but it only made her feel worse. A visit to Willowgate just wouldn't be the same without Holly. Instead she crawled through the hedge and called for Tom, but nobody was home at all. May Days didn't know if Tom was coming to stay and now Tiger wasn't expecting to find anything good at Willowgate.

Early the next morning, the builders arrived and had already begun to put up scaffolding at the front of the house by the time Tiger was dressed. Higher and higher the poles and planks and ladders rose, so that the builders could climb up to the roof to fix the cracked chimney stacks and toppling clay pots. They propped open the conservatory door to let warm air flow through and dry out the damp that was making the bricks crumble. The scaffolding made the house look stronger and straighter, but to Tiger it now felt more skewwhiff than ever without Tom and Holly.

Tiger sighed as May Days rolled up her sleeves and helped carry planks to lay on the platforms. Children were not allowed to climb up the ladder – it was against the rules, the builders said – and Tiger soon wandered off when she felt she was getting in the way. She sat at the kitchen table and drew pictures of tigers and a cat, but the outline of the white cat on a white page wasn't anything like the real thing.

There was a crate in the kitchen, one that May Days had brought from Africa. In the hope of finding something to distract her from waiting for Holly to appear, Tiger leaned over the crate to see what was inside. It was still packed, and there was a small red box on the top that looked interesting.

"May Days!" Tiger called up to the roof. "I found a red wooden box. Can I open it, please? I'll be careful and won't break anything."

"I know you won't," said May Day, smiling down to Tiger. "But that little box contains my most special keepsakes, so I'd like to save showing them to you until we have lots of time to sit down together and I can tell you all about each one."

"OK, but what can I do instead?" said Tiger, a little hurt that all the things she wanted to see were staying hidden – first Holly and now the contents of the red box. From high up, May Days could see her next-door neighbour's car coming

up the lane with an extra passenger.
"Why don't you go and call for Tom
again? I think you might have a nice
surprise!"

Tiger ran round to the hedge at the
back of the house and called for her holiday
friend through the gap underneath.

"Boo!" said Tom, appearing at the other
side and Tiger was so happy to see at least
one of her friends. "Who's up on the
roof?" Tom said.

"Henry and James the builders," said
Tiger. "But somebody else is missing."

Tom crawled through the hedge tunnel
to Tiger.

"A missing person?" asked Tom.

"A missing cat," said Tiger, sighing sadly.
"I can't find Holly."

Did Holly know that they were there,
they wondered? Where could they find her?
Tom screwed up his face, thinking hard.

"I know how we'll find Holly!" said
Tom. "This holiday we can be private-eye
detectives!" He was already crawling out of
the hedge in a hurry. "Come on. Let's get
started!"

"What do we need to be private-eye detectives?" said Tiger, warming to Tom's idea.

"We need to be a bit brave and probably clever," he said.

"We also might need notepads," said Tiger, and then smiled, pleased that her fun friend from next door was there to help.

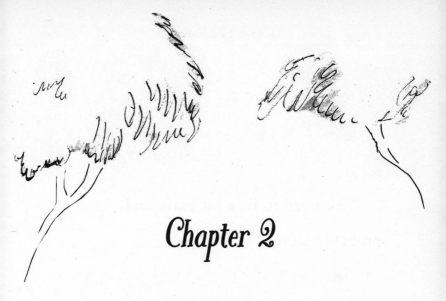

Chapter 2

A Strange Discovery

Tom's grandfather was affectionately known as Grumps, although he was, in fact, the opposite of grumpy. At his kitchen table Tiger and Tom made badges from circles of cardboard and safety pins. On them they wrote: *Private Eye Tiger – Detective*, and *Private Eye Tom – Detective*, shortened to PET detective. It made them think that they were destined to find the cat all along.

"We also need to *feel* like detectives," said Tom to Grumps. "What do they dress like?"

In the back of the cupboard under the stairs, Grumps found a couple of hats, a scarf and a beige-coloured raincoat.

Tom eagerly put on the coat, declaring it an exact fit after he'd hitched it up with the belt. He pinned his badge to the lapel and put on the small brimmed hat.

"That's what Inspector Clouseau would wear," said Grumps with a chuckle, and Tom liked the way the name sounded like *clues*.

"Very Sherlock Holmes!" said Grumps to Tiger as she swished the scarf around

her neck and pinned her badge to the checked hat with ear flaps.

"And might this be of any use?" added Grumps, holding up a magnifying glass that he used for crosswords. Perfect.

Tiger and Tom set off to investigate.

May Days was now helping the builders to carry bricks, two at a time, up to the roof. When Tom saw the scaffolding he immediately wanted to climb up the ladders, but Tiger told him they were not allowed.

"Before you set off," May Day said, smiling at their clever badges and outfits, "there's some clean washing that needs hanging out to dry and I'm too covered in dust to do it myself. Please can you help?"

Tiger and Tom said yes and raced inside to fetch the washing.

The makeshift washing line was looped through pulley-wheels tied between a pillar on the porch and a tree, sagging in the middle where the children could reach. Tiger pegged May Days' shirts and trousers and also a pair of her own tiger-striped socks she'd worn the previous day. With the magnifying glass, Tom inspected the swirls of the skin on his fingertips and then a builder's footprint on the ground.

"You're not helping much," Tiger said.

"I'm looking for clues," Tom said, "but I'm also thinking that what we need is a detective office." They'd wanted to find a den the last time they visited, but hadn't succeeded.

"Good idea! But what we need first

are some detective rules!" said Tiger.

On her notepad, Tiger wrote:

PET detective rules:

1. Find clues and make notes
   about them.
2. Ask questions.
3. Think about the answers.

CASE 1 – The Missing Cat

But so far they hadn't found any clues
and therefore had nothing to write down.
What questions did they need to ask?

Tiger and Tom sat on the lawn and
rubbed their chins, but the only question

they could think of so far was: *where
is Holly?* They definitely needed to be
smarter than this to be detectives.

Tiger squeezed her eyes tight to
see if that would help while Tom
scanned a bare patch of freshly dug
earth with the magnifying glass.

"Look! I've found a paw print!" he said.

"Let me see!" said Tiger, peering closely
at the mark in the soil. "It looks like a cat
paw print! Our first piece of evidence that
Holly has been here."

Tiger drew a copy of the print on the
notepad and Tom poked the ground with
his pencil, digging to see what else was
there.

"Tiger," said Tom slowly, "I think I've found another clue."

"For finding Holly?" Tiger said.

"No, but it might be a strange scientific discovery instead."

Tiger and Tom peered at the moony-coloured shape through the magnifier.

Tom dug away more earth with his pencil and they stared at each other with wide eyes. What Tom had found felt cool and smooth, rounded at one end and pointier at the other. It was an egg. They were sure that birds laid eggs in nests, but this one seemed to have grown in the ground!

"We might have another case already," said Tom.

Together they walked slowly back to the house, with Tiger holding the egg carefully in her hands.

May Days climbed down from the scaffolding as the builders were ready to pack up for the day and go home.

"Oh," she said, seeing the egg. "Is it time for tea, detectives?"

The children explained where they'd found the egg and they all went to the kitchen. Tiger and Tom stared at the evidence, now nestled on the table in a towel to stop it rolling away. They examined it all over with the magnifying glass, but there were no more clues or paw prints.

May Days suggested the children write down a list of animals that they knew laid eggs. Tiger was impressed with Tom's confident guesses.

May Days went through the list and Tiger crossed off the wrong guesses and made some notes.

CASE 2 – The Mysterious Egg
List of Suspects:

~~Dinosaur~~ – Extremely rare.

~~The Easter Bunny~~ – Would be chocolate with foil.

~~Kangaroo~~ – Kangaroos have pouches but don't lay eggs.

~~Turtle~~ – Usually lays lots all together.

~~Lizard~~ – Much smaller eggs.

~~Snake~~ – Not all snakes lay eggs.

Chicken ✓

"If it was a chicken egg from the shops, it would have a little lion and date printed on it," said May Days. "But I declare that it is definitely a chicken egg."

Tiger excitedly put a tick next to the correct answer.

"But how did it get in the ground?" said Tiger.

"Good question!" May Days said with a twinkle in her eye. "And what about this question: *who* might have buried the chicken egg to hide it and save it for their tea another day?"

Tiger and Tom had no idea, but having good questions to think about was very helpful. Tiger took her job as PET detective very seriously and quickly came up with an answer, although not to that particular question.

"Food!" Tiger said, suddenly forgetting

about the egg and going back to case one.
Instead of looking all over for Holly, they
would tempt her to come to them with
food.

Using a box of cat treats, Tiger and Tom
laid a fishy-smelling trail. They scattered
the biscuits from the door, across the lawn
and down towards the part of the garden
that was overgrown and dense, hoping that
wherever Holly was, her clever nose might
bring her back to Willowgate.

Upon investigation the following morning,
Detectives Tiger and Tom found that
the fishy biscuits had gone, which was

a good clue that Holly might have been
there, although they wondered, just for a
moment, if any other animal might have
eaten them too. Unfortunately, there was
no evidence of paw prints on the grass,
though. They also discovered that nobody
had remembered to bring the washing
in from the day before and now Tiger's
striped socks were missing from the line.
And, the conservatory door was left open
overnight and a pot had been broken with
the soil spilled over the floor.

Tom poked around in the soil with his
pencil. There was
another egg buried
there.

But *who* had done all this?

"It must be Holly," said Tom, thinking he had already cracked both cases of the missing cat and mysterious egg (now eggs!). "Holly is an egg and sock thief."

As far as Tom was concerned, there were not two separate investigations but only one. Tiger was upset by two things. If Holly had been there, why hadn't she come to see Tiger? She always used to turn up to see what Tiger was doing. And also, Tiger didn't like her favourite cat being accused of stealing. Tiger rested her pencil against her lips, thinking hard.

"But how could Holly carry the eggs?" she said, trying to picture the cat holding an egg in her paws, or in her mouth, which was hardly big enough. She'd never heard of cats digging holes and burying things. Surely that was not how the eggs got there, and more importantly, Tiger felt sure Holly wouldn't steal.

Tiger wrote down the new developments...

CASE 1: The Missing Cat

Cat biscuits eaten – probably Holly.

Stolen socks – maybe Holly.

Chicken eggs – definitely not Holly because cats can't carry them.

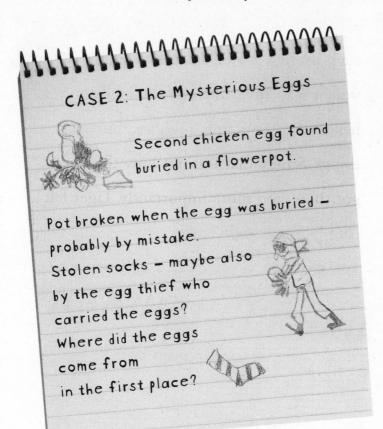

CASE 2: The Mysterious Eggs

Second chicken egg found buried in a flowerpot.

Pot broken when the egg was buried — probably by mistake.

Stolen socks — maybe also by the egg thief who carried the eggs?

Where did the eggs come from in the first place?

These investigations were not finished at all. In fact, they had just become more intriguing. And Tiger wasn't going to let anything distract her from finding Holly, even though May Days' special red box was now in the middle of the kitchen table.

Chapter 3

Who is Twinkle?

Tiger was determined to find Holly.

According to detective rules, questions were essential, and Tiger and Tom decided to conduct some interviews to uncover more information about the missing cat, the mysterious eggs and the stolen socks. Tiger hoped most of all that a clue about either case would lead to finding Holly.

First, Tiger and Tom interviewed May Days.

"When and where was the last time

you saw Holly?" Tiger asked.

"I saw her running down the garden at night, about four days ago."

"Have you seen someone or some*thing* carrying eggs? Or stealing socks?" Tom asked.

"No," said May Days. "I'm afraid I'm not a very good witness."

Tom giggled and assured her she had been an egg-cellent eggs-pert!

Next they interviewed Grumps. He hadn't seen Holly, not for a week. Tiger's tummy felt a little hollow, a bit like a thin eggshell.

"Have you seen someone or some*thing* carrying eggs?" Tiger said.

"Yes," Grumps said. "Me."

"Are you the egg thief?" said Tom.

"Certainly not!" said
Grumps, with a twinkle
in his eye. Neither had he
taken Tiger's socks.

Tiger suggested Tom didn't
jump to any conclusions.

"Mr Grandfather Grumps," said Tiger
politely, "where do you get your eggs?"

"From my neighbours, Mr and Mrs
Cox," Grumps said. "They have chickens
in their garden."

Mr and Mrs Cox lived in a cottage
along the lane and sold eggs from a fold-up
table outside their gate. Grumps needed
some eggs for baking and thought the
children ought to go and pay them a visit.

He also suggested they borrow his old bike to
carry the detective tools that Tom had now
collected: binoculars for a stake-out, gloves to
avoid damaging any evidence or leaving any of
their own fingerprints, a torch for dark and
dusty places, and the magnifying glass.

The bicycle was actually a big creaky
tricycle. It had three wheels, one saddle,

two handles and a large wicker basket
strapped to the front for carrying groceries
or detective equipment. Tom sat on the
saddle and pedalled while Tiger stood on
the bar between the wheels at the back
with her hands on Tom's shoulders. Tiger's
scarf flapped as they whizzed down the
lane to interview new witnesses.

Immediately a clue presented itself
at Mr and Mrs Cox's gate. An egg box
on the table was open. There were only
five eggs inside when there should have
been six. Tom inspected all over with the
magnifying glass but there were no prints.

The children knocked at the house.

"PET detectives, oh, how
useful!" said Mrs Cox,
reading the children's
badges. "But we haven't
lost any chickens."

Tom showed them all the objects in
the basket, explaining what they were
for, and told them that he and Tiger were
investigating a lost cat, some found eggs

and some stolen socks.

"At first we thought it might be a dinosaur egg—" continued Tom, before Tiger interrupted, keen to interview Mr and Mrs Cox.

"Did you know there's an egg missing from the box on your table?"

"Not again!" said Mr Cox. The same thing had happened several times in recent weeks, but they hadn't seen who was doing it.

"Also, have you found a white cat?" Tiger asked. "She's got a wavy tail and is extremely clever."

"Yes, that'll be Twinkle who sometimes visits," said Mr Cox fondly, which made Tiger scowl. "Is she your cat?"

"Her name is *Holly* actually," said Tiger, trying not to pout. She wasn't able to say the cat belonged to her, but it hurt that Holly had found *new* friends. "Holly lives at Willowgate and I miss her."

Mr and Mrs Cox were very sorry, but they hadn't seen the cat for days.

Tom thought that the next job for a detective would be to stake out the eggs to catch the culprit. Mr and Mrs Cox sold them a fresh box of six eggs to take back to Grumps and wished the children luck with solving their cases.

Tiger and Tom hid a little further down the lane behind a hedge with the binoculars trained on the table.

They waited for more than an hour but nobody came for the bait. Tom was such a fidget and wouldn't stop talking about making a detective office and Tiger was feeling quite upset to think that Holly – not *Twinkle!* – wasn't as loyal as she would have liked.

Tom giggled to himself.

"If we see Holly, we could *tail* her," he said, rolling about laughing. Quiet surveillance was not his best skill.

"I want to go now," said Tiger. Nothing seemed funny when the cat she was fond of could so easily forget about her.

Back at Grumps's house, Tiger became more and more anxious that none of the clues were leading her closer to the beloved cat. The children sat at the table in the kitchen to eat the cakes that Grumps had made, but it was hard for Tiger to swallow with a lump in her throat. Had Holly purposefully ignored Tiger because she'd made some better new friends? Was Holly not the friend Tiger thought she was? Tom told some more jokes to cheer up Tiger. He said that he'd thought of a new invention and asked if she'd like to help make it, but Tiger said no. Tom went very quiet then and Tiger trudged back to Willowgate with her heart full of hurt things.

Tiger found May Days in the kitchen and climbed on her lap for comfort and told her she was worried that Holly didn't want to be her friend any more.

"Could you be jumping to conclusions?" asked May Days. "Tom is also a good friend," said May Days, "but when you two are not together are you happy for him to have other friends, so he's not lonely?"

"Yes," said Tiger. "It's just that I'm missing Holly so much..." Tiger's chin trembled.

"Well, maybe Holly misses you as much as you miss her," said May Days, stroking Tiger's hair.

"Do you really think so?" said Tiger hopefully.

Mays Days smiled warmly. "Holly kept going to the gate watching the lane for days after you left last time."

May Days was sure Holly was around somewhere and that there must be a very good reason why she hadn't come to say hello yet.

After a while May Days said, "Are you still interested in my special things in the red box?"

"Yes," said Tiger. "Is today a special day for showing me?"

"Does it feel like a special day?" said May Days.

"Not especially," said Tiger glumly.

"In that case you need to make it one!" said May Days. "So what would be a special day for a detective?"

Tiger smiled for the first time in hours.

"Being clever and finding a really good answer to why Holly hasn't come to see me," said Tiger. "But not on my own."

Tiger decided she wanted to see Tom.

She realised she hadn't been a very good friend earlier and it wasn't fair to make Tom feel bad.

Tiger knew Tom was really just trying to cheer her up when he made a joke about Holly, and she wanted to tell him that she *did* want to help make his invention.

As she went outside, she
heard a bell tinkle. There was
a short step-ladder in front of the beech
tree that hadn't been there before, and
a bell was ringing up in the branches.
Tiger climbed up to see what it was.
Tied to a branch was an old washing line
looped through a pulley-wheel. The
line went over the hedge and all the way
up to Tom's bedroom window. Hanging
from the line was a peg-bag with a bell
sewn on and a note pegged to it.

So this was the invention Tom wanted
to build! Tiger reached for the note and
read it:

Dear Tiger,
    Sorry if my jokes are not funny.
Here's a better one that Grumps told
me. Why did the rooster cross the
road? To cockadoodledooo something.
Hope it makes you laugh.
    From your holiday friend, Detective
Tom.
    P.S. Grumps helped me invent the
Peg-Bag-Pulley. You can send me a
message if you like.

Tiger laughed to herself, glad that they
both had grandparents to help them.

She wrote a note back to Tom, attached it to the bag and then pulled the line so that the Peg-Bag-Pulley went all the way back to Tom's bedroom. The bell rang in the distance as it stopped at the other end. Tiger's note said:

Dear Tom,

Your jokes are very funny and you never make me feel sad, only lost cats do. Please would you still be my PET detective partner tomorrow?

From your holiday friend, Detective Tiger.

P.S. The Peg-Bag-Pulley is an egg-cellent invention!

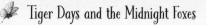

"How did your whole day turn out?" May Days asked later that evening. "Was anything special?"

"Some of it wasn't very happy and lots of it was, but I think tomorrow already feels like it's going to be a special day." Before going to bed, Tiger scattered some more cat biscuits at the front of the house... just in case.

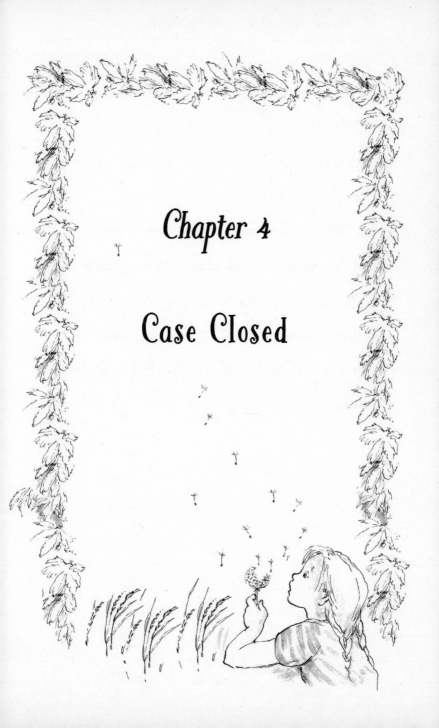

Chapter 4

Case Closed

Tiger woke up with a feeling that today would be a good day for thinking cleverly with her friend Tom. Tom wanted to continue investigating the case of the Mysterious Eggs and Stolen Socks. He still thought Holly should be on the list of suspects for both thefts, for now, because of the cat paw print they'd found near the egg in the ground. Tiger agreed they should keep working on all

the cases, feeling absolutely sure that a
clue from either one would definitely
lead to solving the most important case of
all – finding Holly.

Tiger also added two new rules to the
PET detective list, so now there were five:

1. Find clues and make notes about
   them.
2. Ask questions.
3. Think about the answers.
4. Find good reasons for the answers.
5. Don't jump to conclusions.

"And we still need a detective office.
I think we should make one in the Staring
Oat Shed!" said Tom.

"Not the Staring Oat Shed again,"
sighed Tiger. They'd been there before to
try to make a den. The old shed was dark
and dusty and Tiger was afraid of the great
big monster called the Staring Oat that
Tom said lived there. With bright green
eyes, it would stare at you so hard that it
made you dizzy and fall over.

"All we have to do is go down there
and defeat the monster first," said Tom
bravely.

"How do you know the Staring
Oat definitely lives in the shed?" Tiger
wondered.

"I saw it at Willowgate ages ago when
I was staying with Grumps," said Tom. It

was long before he'd met Tiger. Once, he and Grumps had been watching for bats at night and Tom had seen the frightful eyes glaring back at him through the binoculars. "We used to come in the garden sometimes before May Days moved in."

If Tom had seen the Staring Oat then that made him an eye-witness and meant that the monster was real.

"We're detectives," said Tom, trying to encourage Tiger. "We need to find clues, search in places where nobody goes and interview witnesses." He gasped. "What if… the Staring Oat has kidnapped Holly?!"

Tiger was afraid of the Staring Oat, but she would do anything to find Holly. Tiger took a deep breath and said, "OK, but if we're going to meet the Staring Oat, then we need armour." Something that would make them seem bigger and stronger than Tiger felt.

Like detective knights on horseback, Tom pedalled on the tricycle and Tiger stood behind him. With one hand on Tom's shoulder, Tiger held out a long broom with stiff bristles in front of them and Tom tied a tray to his arm as a shield for protection. Slowly the tricycle flattened a path through the long grass and into the great unexplored part of the garden.

As they got closer to the shed, they found two good clues. Lying on the ground, a little dirty and crumpled, were Tiger's stolen socks.

"Our best clue yet!" said Tom. "This must be the right way to find the thief."

Tiger picked up the socks and inspected them with the magnifier. There were lots of small holes and tears in them.

"Holly's claws?" said Tom. "Or the Staring Oat's teeth?"

"Holly definitely didn't steal the socks," said Tiger.

"How can you be sure?" said Tom.

Tiger made Tom look closely through the magnifier. "Hairs!" They weren't white like Holly's fur. They were orange.

"What colour is the Staring Oat?" gulped Tiger.

Tom shrugged. "I only saw its glowing eyes."

On they went, even more slowly and cautiously now.

Next they found some eggshells. Wide-eyed, Tiger and Tom now knew they were on the right track and Tom pedalled hard, pushing through the long grass. But what were they going to find?

"Stop!" whispered Tiger, when she saw the shed above the tall grass.

"Remember, don't look into the Staring Oat's eyes," said Tom.

They climbed off the tricycle and parted the grass to crouch and peep. There, in a small clearing, was what they had searched for and hoped to find. Holly! Tiger was about to jump up when Tom caught her scarf and pulled her down.

"Someone else is there," he whispered, and they stayed hidden in case it was the monster.

Holly waved her tail in the air, her ears pricked as she looked off to the side where the grasses were rustling and twitching. Holly was not alone, but she hadn't been kidnapped by the Staring Oat. Holly pounced, and out from the grasses leapt another creature. Orange-coloured, with a triangular face and ears and a long bushy tail tipped in white, a fox was playing hide-and-seek with Holly.

Enormously relieved to find the adored cat, Tiger couldn't bear it any longer. "Holly!" she called happily, springing out from the grasses and running over to be reunited with her other holiday friend. "I missed you so much, Holly Days!" she said, holding the soft white cat in her arms who purred and purred, while the startled fox slipped quickly under the shed.

"May Days!" Tiger called up to the roof. "We found Holly!"

May Days came down from the roof on hearing the good news and they all went to the kitchen. Tiger and Tom gabbled the whole story about how they found Holly playing with a fox. May Days had left a nature book on the table with the pages left open on wildlife footprints. Tiger identified the pawprint they'd found in the earth by the first egg. It wasn't from a cat, it was from a fox.

Tom pointed to the picture of the fox that had a long triangular nose and a mouth that was much bigger than a cat's.

"I think we finally have proof that it was the fox who stole and buried the eggs, as well as stealing the socks," said Tiger. She looked at Holly, who sat beside the egg, still nestled in a cloth on the table, patting it gently with her paw to see if she could make it roll. Tiger still wasn't comfortable thinking of any creature as a thief, though.

The children thought they ought to tell Mr and Mrs Cox about the fox, so they set off down the drive on the tricycle. Holly didn't want to sit in the basket but was happy to race alongside them, back with her old friends again.

Mr and Mrs Cox were pleased to see Holly too. They stroked her but she went straight back to winding herself round Tiger's legs, rolling on her back and letting Tiger tickle her tummy.

Tiger explained Holly had made friends with a fox, which was probably why nobody else had seen much of her.

She and Tom showed them the holey

socks, the wildlife book and the egg shells,

proof that the fox had been the culprit.

Mr and Mrs Cox said their chickens had

always been safe from the fox in their coop

and run, but the eggs for sale would now

be stored in a cool box with a lid.

CASE 1: The Missing Cat

Holly found near the
Staring Oat Shed playing
with a fox.

CASE CLOSED

CASE 2: The Mysterious Eggs
(and the Stolen Socks)

The eggs belonged to Mr and Mrs Cox.
The fox has a long nose and mouth.
The fox ~~stole~~ took the eggs and the
socks, which means the fox broke
the flowerpot but nobody minds.

CASE CLOSED

"Why do you think the fox went under the shed?" May Days asked.

"Because it's made a den there," said Tiger. Tom slumped a little huffily over the table.

"But the shed was supposed to be our detective office," he said, with his nose in May Days' wildlife book, although he admitted that he admired the clever fox for being bold enough to make a den beneath the Staring Oat Shed.

"Why aren't Holly or the fox afraid of the Staring Oat?" said Tiger.

"A good question for PET detectives," said May Days. "And I think you are just *beginning* to make an important discovery about the fox."

"Is it because foxes are brave?" said Tom, wrinkling his unsure nose. Could you be a thief and brave at the same time?

"Or, maybe the Staring Oat isn't there," said Tiger. "Maybe… it's gone on holiday!"

Just like Tiger and Tom came to stay for the holidays, maybe the Staring Oat went away to stay with someone else too. Did Staring Oats have grandparents?

Nothing could be answered just yet – they would have to do some more detective work tomorrow. Tiger and Tom wanted to be sure that while the fox was living under the shed it was safe and undisturbed. Tom asked if he could borrow the wildlife book to see if he could find out any more useful information and Tiger opened a new case in their notebook:

CASE 3: Where is the Staring Oat?

Do Staring Oats have families?

That evening Tiger sat on May Days' lap,
with Holly on hers, saying she'd had a very
special day as she was back with her
treasured cat. Intrigued and excited about
the new investigation she would pursue
tomorrow, Tiger felt quite content.

"When I find out the important discovery about the fox, will you show me your special things?" Tiger said, as solving the case of the missing cat and the case of the mysterious eggs (and stolen socks) seemed reward enough for one day.

Yes, May Days would love to share her own important things when the time was right.

Chapter 5

Rules of Being a Fox

Tiger was excited and up early. The builders had just arrived and they had left their bag of sandwiches on the windowsill of the house while their hands were full carrying tools up to the roof. Tiger froze in her tracks. The fox was slinking stealthily across the lawn.

The fox didn't see Tiger and, standing on its hind legs with its front paws up on the windowsill, sniffed curiously at the lunch bag.

89

Then, without hesitating, it snatched the bag in its mouth and trotted off down the garden with the prize while the builders' backs were turned!

Although the fox had only been there for half a minute, it seemed like a special treat to see it, even though it had run off with the lunch. But Tiger worried about the fox getting into trouble for taking the lunch, and the fact that it might run into the Staring Oat. Any friend of Holly's was now her friend too, so Tiger added some extra questions to the case to investigate:

CASE 3: Where is The Staring Oat?

Do Staring Oats have families?

Will the fox be safe if the Staring Oat comes back?

Has anyone else seen the Staring Oat?

Tiger wrote a short note – *Hurry up and get out of bed, Detective Tom!* – and sent it to Tom in the Peg-Bag-Pulley. She heard the bell in the distance, when it jingled against his window and, before long, Tom arrived in his detective raincoat and hat.

Tiger first wanted to find out if the builders liked foxes before she told them who had taken their lunch. Tiger and Tom prepared a replacement lunch by making some cheese and crisp sandwiches and pouring glasses of lemonade, bobbing with apple chunks and ice cubes.

The new witnesses

were called Henry and James, father and son, and they were just coming down with May Days from the scaffolding for lunch. They were impressed by the children's badges and the cases they had already solved.

With notepad ready, Tiger asked them some questions:

"While you have been working up on the roof, did you see a big scary creature with glaring, glowing eyes?"

No, unfortunately – or was it fortunately? – they hadn't.

"Do you like foxes?" Tiger asked nervously.

"Foxes are a nuisance," said Henry gruffly. "They steal things from our bin at home and make a mess with the rubbish all over the lawn."

Tiger squeezed her mouth tight, feeling quite protective about Holly's friend, the fox.

"We're very sorry to tell you," said Tom, seeing Tiger about to get upset, "a fox stole your lunch."

"The fox didn't know that it was stealing, or that eggs and socks and sandwiches belong to other people!" said Tiger hurriedly.

"We made you another lunch," Tom added.

The children waited to see what Henry would say now.

"Maybe I've been lucky to have my lunch taken," said Henry, enjoying the treats the children had made.

James agreed, saying, "This is a much better lunch than the one we prepared. The fox is also lucky to have you to defend it."

May Days smiled brightly at the children.

"We're going to protect the fox from the Staring Oat," said Tiger bravely.

"We'd better go now," said Tom hurriedly. "We've got a den to stake out. The Staring Oat might be coming back any minute."

The stakeout at the Staring Oat Shed was as boring as staking out Mr and Mrs Cox's eggs. Nothing to do but be still and quiet, camouflaged by grasses sticking out of their hats, lying on their fronts and waiting. Holly was much better at it than the children as she curled up and snoozed in the dry grass beside them. They didn't see the Staring Oat or the fox at all. Feeling disappointed that they had no leads, Tiger and Tom trudged back to their grandparents' houses.

May Days' little red keepsake box was open on the kitchen table in front of her. She asked Tiger to sit beside her as she had something to show her.

"I didn't know today was a special day," said Tiger, "because I haven't found out what the other important discovery is yet."

"It certainly was a special day. Today my granddaughter learned that foxes can't help being foxes, no matter what people think of them."

Without letting Tiger look inside, May Days pulled out something small and put it in Tiger's hand. Made from silver, it was a tiny tiger charm from a bracelet.

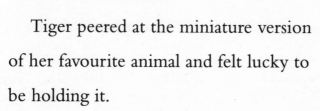

Tiger peered at the miniature version of her favourite animal and felt lucky to be holding it.

"Your parents bought that for me when

97

you were born as I was so far away in Africa and missed the whole special event of you arriving in the world," May Days said. "I didn't get to see you, but I had this to remind me of you."

Tiger would have liked to wear the charm herself, but it was her grandmother's special thing, and she gave it back, now warmed from her own hands.

"Are there more things in your box?" Tiger asked.

"There are," smiled May Days, "but I'll share those with you another special day."

Perhaps it had been a surprising day

more than anything. Foxes were surprising, and so was Holly, and Staring Oats were more difficult to find than both of them. Just before Tiger got into bed, Holly took off, running down the garden into the night, instead of curling up on Tiger's feet like a furry hot-water bottle.

"It's bedtime!" Tiger called after Holly, disappointed she didn't stay. "We've finished playing for the day." Had Holly gone to say goodnight to the fox? Would they be safe from the Staring Oat?

Tiger tried not to worry and instead thought about the other discovery still to make about the fox. She wrote a note to Tom saying she thought they still didn't

know enough about foxes and sent it to him on the Peg-Bag-Pulley.

Two minutes later a note came tinkling back.

Don't worry! Detective Tom is already on the case!

Tiger smiled – she could always rely on Tom to help.

Chapter 6

From Up on
the Roof

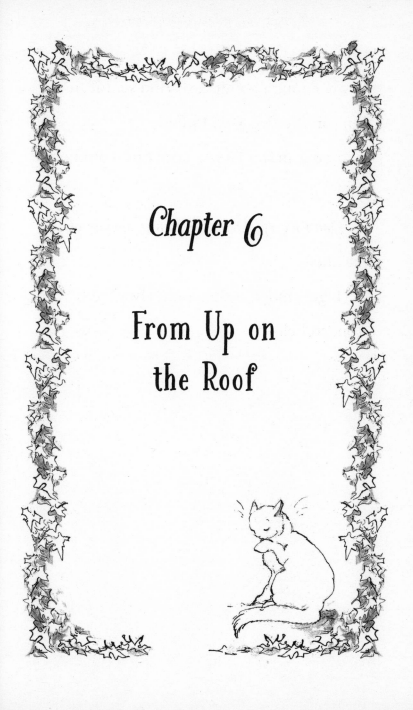

The clanking and clumping of the builders' boots on the ladders and scaffolding woke Tiger. Holly was asleep on Tiger's feet, although Tiger hadn't noticed her come back during the night.

Tiger got up and Holly lazily opened her eyes but then went back to sleep, waving her tail and then curling it round her paws, still damp from the night dew.

Tiger put on her wellies and detective

hat and crept across the grass. There were no sandwiches on the windowsill and the fox wasn't about, but someone whispered her name.

"Detective Tiger?" said James the builder, as quietly as he could from the top of the scaffolding. "I can see the fox from here!"

Still in her pyjamas, Tiger went to the
Peg-Bag-Pulley and sent a note ringing at
the other end of the line.

> Detective Tom!
> Wake Up!
> Fox spotted!
> Come Quickly!

James was still up on the roof, pointing
in the direction they should take, when
Tom appeared in pyjamas and detective
raincoat. Tiger and Tom crept swiftly and
quietly towards the Staring Oat Shed, but
were only just in time to see the white tip
of the fox's tail disappearing through the

grasses and
then into
its den.

James was waiting for the children when they came back. He'd been watching the fox from the rooftop for a little while. He had a good view of the den from the roof and it was far enough away so that the fox didn't know it was being watched. James did like foxes, even though his dad wasn't so sure.

"But it's not fair," said Tiger. "If we're not allowed up on the roof, we can't stake out the Staring Oat Shed, *and* we'll keep missing the fox."

Over breakfast Tiger and Tom tried to think of ways to convince the builders, Mays Days and Grumps to let them up on the roof too. May Days plopped a boiled

egg and a slice of toast on to their plates
and said that the rules were there for a
good reason and that a building site was a
dangerous place for children.

Tom frowned. Nothing seemed to be
going his way: no office, no good sightings
of the fox, no Staring Oat to defeat, and he
had now begun to feel tired and unwell.
His throat and head hurt and his nose was
running.

Grumps came to collect him, although
Tom was unhappy to go.

"It's only a cold and if you rest and take
some medicine you will probably be well
enough to join in again soon," Grumps
said firmly.

"I really want to find out where the Staring Oat is, and to see the fox again," said Tom, looking sadder than Tiger had ever seen him before. He let out a big sigh as Grumps took him home to rest.

Tiger felt bad for Tom and sat quietly at the table doing a lot of important thinking. Suddenly she had a bright idea that might solve all the things Tom was disappointed about at once.

"What about if we build a high-up detective office instead!" she said, and cracked the top of her egg with a teaspoon.

They would need everybody's help.

May Days thought it was a brilliant idea and chose a suitable wide-spreading oak tree in the garden.

Tiger drew a treehouse den and
then showed her plan to the builders
and politely asked if they had any spare
scaffolding planks
that she could
borrow. The two
builders looked at
the design and said
they had enough spare pieces and would
build it in no time at all during their lunch
break and after work.

Tiger and May Days called at Grumps's
house that evening. May Days gave Tom

a bunch of grapes and Tiger gave him a
puzzle book and some cards to play with.
Tiger tried to show Tom how to play
Patience. After only one afternoon, Tom
was already going crazy stuck in his room.

"How will we know if the Staring Oat
comes back?" asked Tom. "What about
protecting the fox?" Tom was impatient to
be outside, detecting again.

"The Staring Oat is lucky you're
unwell," said Tiger to make him feel better,
"otherwise you would definitely defeat it."

Tom wanted to get out of bed.

"Tom! You'd better not get up," said Tiger,
who didn't want to spoil the treehouse
surprise until it was completely finished.

With a firm voice, Grumps said, "Back into bed, young man. Quiet and rest. Those are the rules."

"Rules are boring," said Tom. His eyes were watery and his nose red. Perhaps he wasn't quite up to doing what he thought he could do, and suddenly he felt very sleepy.

"Get better soon, Tom," said Tiger.

It had been a long day for Tiger building the treehouse, which had safety ropes all round it and a strong wooden floor that she'd helped to nail down. Tiger had promised to be very careful and grown-up when in the treehouse so, after she'd helped to fix the wooden ladder, she was allowed to be the first to climb up and look out at the great unexplored garden. It felt wonderful to see the view of the Staring Oat Shed from between the branches, but would feel even more special when Tom felt better and was standing next to her.

Back in the tent and nearly time for bed, May Days had her red box with her.

"I had some special friends in Africa," she said, opening the lid. "They gave me these beads when I left."

May Days pulled out strings of

coloured beads and placed them over Tiger's head. The colours were joyful and bright. Sometimes when she missed her life back on the wildlife reserve in Africa, May Days would wear the beads and it would remind her of happy days with old friends.

"But it wasn't a special day today," said Tiger. "It was a feeling-a-bit-lost-without-my-friend-Tom day."

"You've been a good friend to Tom," said May Days, "and that made it special."

Tiger swished the beads and they tickled as they rolled across her neck. She wanted to make sure the fox and Holly were safe from the Staring Oat, hoping Tom would get better soon so they could watch out for them from their new high-up detective office.

"I want to be the fox's friend too," said Tiger very thoughtfully.

May Days said she was very proud of Tiger for saying this.

"Is there anything else in the box to show me?" Tiger asked.

"Just one more thing," May Days chuckled.

Tiger was determined to make tomorrow the most special day of all. Tiger was allowed to wear the joyous beads for a little longer before returning them to May Days to keep safely in her red box.

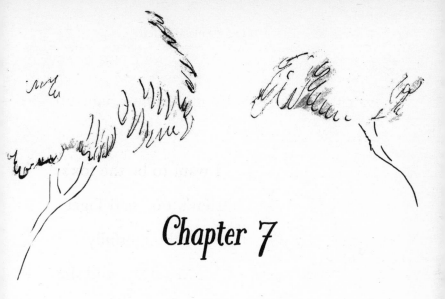

Chapter 7

The Real Discovery

The next morning Grumps told Tiger that Tom still needed to stay resting in bed for the day.

The builders would finish rebuilding the chimney stacks by the following day, and once they were done, they would take all the scaffolding away again. That included the pieces borrowed for the treehouse. There wasn't much time.

Tiger was more determined than ever

to make sure she and Tom could protect
their friends, Holly and the fox. She wrote
a list of the things she and Tom would
need for a very special stakeout. She wrote
a note for Tom and was about to send it
to him on the Peg-Bag-Pulley when she
noticed there was already a note waiting
for her.

Dear Tiger
It's nearly midnight but I woke
up and read the book about foxes,
using my torch. Foxes mostly come out
of their dens at night which is why
we haven't seen it much. They have
good night vision and their eyes glow
green when you shine a light in them.
From your friend, Tom.

Tiger smiled to herself. Not everyone slept at the same time and that must be the reason Holly didn't stay on the camp bed at night, and why she was sleepy in the daytime. Maybe the Staring Oat only came out at night too! Tiger put her own note in the Peg-Bag-Pulley, asking Tom to follow some rules she had made for him. They were good rules to help him get well:

Dear Tom,
Today you have to sleep and rest and be quiet. If you do and feel better, there will be a surprise for you tonight.
Your friend, Tiger.
P.S. I can't solve the case of 'Where is the Staring Oat' without you.

She signed it with a tiny tiger picture, coloured in with a silver pencil, just like the charm from May Days' bracelet.

A little later, she went to see Grumps again, who was tiptoeing around the house so that he didn't disturb Tom.

"Do you think Tom will be well enough to come out this evening, just for a little while?" Tiger whispered.

"Perhaps, but I don't think he'll be able to do too much," whispered Grumps.

"He doesn't have to do anything except watch. It's a night-time stakeout," giggled Tiger. "You and May Days have to come too."

In more whispers, she asked Grumps if he would help her make a toy from an old tiger-print sock. She'd stuffed it with some dry grass but didn't know how to sew it closed.

"What is it for?" whispered Grumps.

"For a new friend," said Tiger.

While Grumps sewed up the ends of the sock, also darning tiger eyes and whiskers on the toe, Tiger heard the quiet snores of Tom healing in his sleep in the bedroom down the hall. There was so much to do, but Tiger had only her friends in mind, and that really did make it feel like the most special day for her too.

"Wakey, wakey, Detective Holly, you are going to have to be my detective partner today," Tiger said. "I'm not going on my own." Holly stretched and yawned and jumped off the camp bed and Tiger hopped on the tricycle with a box of cat biscuits and the sock toy in the basket.

Holly and Tiger went down towards the Staring Oat Shed. When they were quite close, Tiger got off the tricycle and crouched down, scared at being so close to the monster's den without Tom by her side. Still thinking of her friend, and with Holly tucked under one arm, she stepped out into the clearing, scattering the biscuits and sock toy, before jumping back

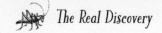

on the tricycle and cycling away at speed.

There was still lots of work to do in the treehouse too...

The sun dipped behind the trees that evening and left the sky dark blue. Tom was sitting up in bed, bored stiff from having to be indoors all day, when Tiger arrived wearing pyjamas and a dressing gown, and her detective hat and badge.

"Did you follow my rules?" Tiger said.

"I did, and I feel much better now," said Tom.

"Your PET detective taxi is here to take you somewhere special," said Tiger.

Tom was thrilled and excited, as he hadn't expected to be able to go outside. He almost leapt from the bed before Grumps slowed him down. Wrapped in his warm dressing gown and wearing the detective raincoat and hat, Tom was shown to the tricycle that now had a cushion in the bottom of the big wicker basket.

"Climb in!" said Tiger.

With Tom's legs hanging out, Tiger

pedalled and Grumps helped to push. Out of the front gate they went, and down the lane to Willowgate.

A lantern burned brightly on the gatepost.

"We have to be very quiet, Tom," said Tiger. "This is the most important rule." He said he'd try his best.

More lanterns and candles lit a path to the treehouse. Tiger had made it into a comfy den for them all, spread with blankets and pillows against the trunk so Tom could lie back. There were snacks and flasks of hot chocolate, and Holly and May Days were waiting for them for their evening stakeout.

The night drew in and the moon rose.
They were now high enough to look right
over the overgrown jungle garden to the
clearing in front of the shed.

Nobody found it boring staking out the
Staring Oat Shed, warmed by hot chocolate
and excited whispers. Suddenly Tom froze,
dropping the binoculars
from his nose.

"S-S-Staring Oat!"
he spluttered, trying not
to make too much noise.
"I just saw it under the shed!"

Alarmed for the fox, Tiger grabbed the
binoculars. Huge, glowing, bright green
eyes reflected the moon and lamplight

like mirrors. Tiger lowered the binoculars and now the glowing eyes seemed much smaller.

"The binoculars magnify the eyes, Tom!" Had Tom jumped to another conclusion all that time ago? Tiger handed the binoculars back to Tom, hoping that he would solve this case himself. What else had glow-in-the-dark eyes?

"Wait a minute!" whispered Tom, as just then he spotted two triangle ears, a black shiny nose and the orange fur round the eyes. "It's not the Staring Oat's eyes, it's the fox's!"

Holly suddenly turned tail, bouncing carefully down the wooden ladder steps and disappeared into the bushes. As everyone's eyes grew accustomed to the dim light, they too could make out the triangular shapes of the fox's ears and nose, as it pawed at the ground to find the biscuits in the grass.

"I think we've found the *real* Staring Oat!" giggled Tiger.

The fox found the sock toy, sniffed it, picked it up in its mouth and then dropped it again, just outside the den. Everyone stayed very still and quiet, but suddenly Holly jumped out of the grass to play hide-and-seek with the fox again. Holly was so lucky to be a cat and get so close.

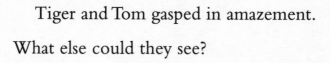

Tiger and Tom gasped in amazement. What else could they see?

Two more triangular noses followed by four glowing eyes and eight more paws, came out from under the shed. Two fox cubs!

Tiger and Tom had to stop themselves from shrieking with delight and stay quiet. They felt very fortunate to see what they could see.

Soon growing confident, the fox cubs trotted out of the shadows and picked up each end of the sock toy, pulling it and pouncing around. Their fur looked softer and fluffier and they were a much rounder shape than the mother fox.

Tiger wished she could be close enough to touch them as they rolled and tumbled over each other, diving, leaping, bounding and ambushing one another.

Nobody in the tree den needed to ask each other to be quiet or stay still now as they were all mesmerised by the fox cubs and their mother and a white cat, playing in the light of the moon

and lamps. There was nothing to say
and only joy to feel at what they had all
discovered together.

CASE 3: Where is the Staring Oat?

It never existed!

CASE COMPLETELY SOLVED.

Chapter 8

Rare Friendships

Tom was leaving to go home before Tiger. He was looking forward to telling his friends back at school about his stay at Grumps's house, how he'd found a dinosaur egg, defeated a monster and discovered a family of foxes.

"The fox cubs will have grown up by the time it's summer holidays and they'll leave home and go and find their own dens somewhere else," said Tom. He'd learned a lot about foxes and shared what he knew. "Then we can find out what it's really like inside the shed!"

Tiger wasn't sure if it should be a detective office now all their cases were solved. Perhaps they'd wait and see what new adventure they might have the next time they saw each other. Tiger and Tom said a hundred goodbyes and Tiger waved with Grumps from his gate.

Tiger was in the garden with Holly when May Days came to find her.

"I have one last thing to show you before you go home," she said.

The last keepsake in the little red wooden box.

May Days first told Tiger how impressed she was with the way she and Tom had respected the foxes, and how they had abandoned the idea of a detective's office in the shed while the space underneath was occupied. Tiger truly was a friend to the foxes. Because of this, May Days would show Tiger something she had never shown anyone in England.

It was a surprise to find that the last special keepsake was a small, smooth, soapstone carving of a rhinoceros.

"Why is this special?" Weren't tigers May Days' favourite animal as well as Tiger's?

"A long time ago, while I was in Africa," May Days began, "I found a young injured rhinoceros, all alone…"

In pain, afraid and hungry, it wasn't easy to help such a large baby. Rhinoceroses, like many wild animals, were uneasy around people. With the help of friends who cared about wild animals, May Days had managed to look after the poor rhino on the reserve until it was old enough and strong enough to survive on its own. They tried not to interfere too much as Wilfred grew. By the time he was released back into the wild, he was one of only a few of his kind left in the world.

"I called him Wilfred," May Days said. "And although he was rough-skinned and terrifyingly big when he was fully grown, I loved him like a friend."

Tiger blinked, amazed.

"That's when I met a young lady called Grace. She was courageous and that made her clever," May Days continued. "You remind me very much of her. Grace became one of the rangers in the reserve helping to protect Wilfred in the wild from people who don't understand how beautiful rhinos are."

"Beautiful?" Tiger said, unsure, thinking

of their tiny eyes and clumpy legs, rectangle
heads and thin twitchy tufts of tails.

"Once you make friends with a
rhinoceros, you find they are very
beautiful indeed," said May Days.
"Remember when Henry said he thought
foxes were a nuisance?"

Tiger nodded.

"Well, he told me before he left
that you have helped him to change
his mind and see how lovely foxes are.

That's a wonderful thing."

Tiger blushed quietly as May Days continued her story.

Occasionally over the years May Days had spotted Wilfred in the wild. She was happiest when she saw her dear friend doing the things that rhinos do, even if he was charging and bellowing and stamping his foot. Grace was keeping an eye on Wilfred now, and May Days felt confident that he was safe.

"I've been lucky to watch Wilfred, from a distance, being a wild rhino," May Days said.

"I feel the same about the foxes," Tiger smiled.

"And I feel the same about you," May Days chuckled.

 141

The scaffolding had gone, and although
the chimney stacks and pots were tall and
straight now, Willowgate House once again
looked slightly skewwhiff and somehow,
the house also seemed like an old friend
that Tiger hadn't seen for a while.

Before Tiger returned Grumps's tricycle
she had one more visit she wanted to

make. She set off down the lane with
Holly running alongside. Mr and Mrs Cox
were pleased to see them both.

Tiger told them about Holly and the
cubs and that she and the cat were friends
to the foxes. Mr and Mrs Cox agreed to
leave a spare egg out now and again, just
in case the foxes needed them.

"And please would you still keep an eye on Holly when I'm not here?" Tiger asked.

Of course they would.

"I think I prefer Holly as her name," said Mr Cox. "Twinkle doesn't quite suit such a clever, independent cat."

Tiger said goodbye then cycled over to Grumps's to return the tricycle and ask him if he would also keep an eye out for Holly while Tiger wasn't there.

"Holly needs friends when I'm not around," said Tiger.

Of course he would, and Tiger was happy that Holly would have lots of friends to visit.

When Mr Days arrived, Tiger took him
down into the overgrown garden to show
him where the fox den was. They were
delighted when six shining eyes and three
pointed noses poked out. It was so nice to
share seeing the fox and cubs with her dad.
Even that small moment seemed incredibly
big and special.

"The treehouse was here," said
Tiger, pointing at the oak tree, "and the
scaffolding on the house was over there."
But everything had gone now.

"It all looks the same as it did when I
dropped you off," said Mr Days. He held

Tiger's hands and said, "Except for two small bright things."

"I know – aren't we lucky to have seen fox cubs!"

"I meant my daughter's eyes," said Mr Days. "They seem to be shining with something brave and clever and beautiful."

May Days waved and blew kisses from the porch and Holly followed the car down to the gate where Tiger jumped out to open and then close it behind them after Mr Days drove through. Holly jumped up on the gatepost.

"Have a lovely time until I next visit," said Tiger to Holly.

Please be here when I come back, wished

Tiger, wondering what other unexpected things she might find at Willowgate next time. Holly watched Tiger being driven away, her tail unfurling and curling over the sign Tiger had made for the gate...

ALL VISITORS
TO WILLOWGATE
MUST BE FRIENDS
TO THE FOXES.

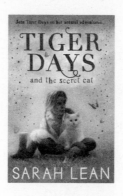

Read an extract from Tiger Days'
first adventure at Willowgate House.

Tiger Days didn't know anyone who loved tigers as much as she did.

She wore tiger pyjamas, socks and slippers, and spent a lot of time in her bedroom reading about tigers and drawing tiger pictures. Her parents would often suggest bike rides and trips to the swimming pool on Saturday afternoons, but Tiger would much rather be in her bedroom doing tiger things.

One Saturday afternoon, her parents
appeared at her door.

"You'll never guess who that was on
the phone…" said Mum.

"Hmmmm?" said Tiger, not really
listening.

Dad rolled his eyes as Tiger's nose
stayed firmly buried in her wildlife book.
"It was May Days!" he said.

Tiger looked up, surprised.
May Days was her
grandmother and had
been living in Africa
on a wildlife reserve
since Tiger was a baby.

Whenever May Days phoned, Tiger asked when she was coming to visit, but May Days said it was hard to know because the giraffes or rhinos always needed her more. This time, May Days had phoned with wonderful news. She had finally come back to England and bought a place called Willowgate House.

"She wants you to go and stay," said Dad. "You can have your first adventure together at the new house."

Tiger wrinkled her nose. She was sometimes nervous about doing new things and the idea of a real-life adventure with May Days was a little scary. She had a feeling May Days wasn't going to be like everyone else's grandmother.

"Won't you be worried about me?" she asked her parents.

"While you're with May Days? Not even for a second," said Mum, although it was obvious that *somebody* was worried.

But Tiger put on a brave smile for her

parents. An adventure with May Days would be great, wouldn't it?

"Are you sure this is the right house?" said Tiger.

She stood close to her dad by the gate, beneath a large drooping willow tree.

Willowgate House was unexpectedly huge, and it stood at the end of a long driveway. It had wide windows and tall chimney pots, and a conservatory that leaned slightly to the left.

Tiger tilted her head to the side to see if it looked any straighter. But it didn't. The lopsided building made her feel wobbly.

Tiger waited on the doorstep behind Dad while he pulled the bell on the wall beside the door.

The next surprise was May Days.

Weren't grandmothers supposed to be old and grey and worn?

Instead she had curls that were wild and alive. Her sleeves were pushed up, as if she'd done a hard day's work, and she bounded out like the kind of person who didn't sit down very often.

"You're here, at last!" May Days beamed, throwing her arms around Dad first, and then around Tiger. Tiger peered behind her grandmother at the bare floorboards and curved staircase in

the hall. It looked as if nobody had lived

here for a very long time.

"You were no bigger than a koala

the last time I saw you," May Days said,

holding Tiger by the cheeks. Tiger blinked
in surprise, and her tummy did a flip.

"You've got a big house," said Tiger,
not sure what else to say.

"Too big for one person," May
Days said, chuckling like a barrel full of
chickens. "Come in! Come in!"

Mr Days had also not seen his mother
for a very long time and he had lots to
tell her over gallons of tea. They laughed
and talked while Tiger sat on a chair, still
clinging to her tiger-striped suitcase. The
faded lino flooring curled up in the corners
of the kitchen, and there wasn't a lot more

to see than an old cooking range and a long pine table that had worn into a curve in the middle. Where were the proper kitchen cupboards and worktops? Tiger hoped that the rest of the house had been decorated.

"Thank you for bringing me my granddaughter," May Days said, squeezing Mr Days' cheeks when he had to leave.

Tiger clung to her dad for an extra-long hug.

"Are you sure you don't need me at home?" Tiger whispered.

"We'll miss you terribly," said Mr Days, "but you and your grandmother have a lot of catching-up to do."

"It's just you and me," said May Days, after they'd waved the car into the distance.

"Shall I put my things in my room?" said Tiger.

"Your room?" said May Days, smiling. "You'd better come with me."

May Days showed Tiger the outside bathroom first. Although the walls and floor were bare brick, there were soft towels, a cup for toothbrushes, a mirror and a light bulb with a long pull cord, all sparkling clean. Tiger tried to smile brightly.

"I'm afraid we haven't got a shower or bath yet," said May Days. "But I have spare flannels if you need one."

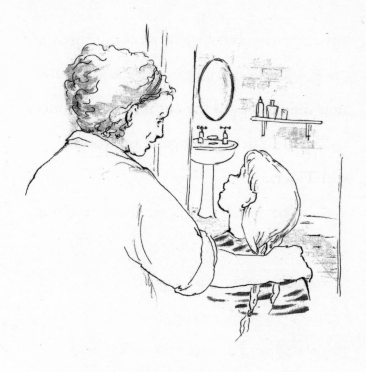

She turned Tiger's shoulders to face
the back garden. "We're going to share a
room."

Tiger would have her own room one
day, May Days assured her, but all of
Willowgate needed a lot of work first.

For now, they were going to be staying in the garden in an old green tent.

A tent? thought Tiger, her eyes wide. *Outside?!*